# Thomas-saurus Rex

Illustrated by Richard Courtney
A Random House PICTUREBACK® Book

## Random House New York

Thomas the Tank Engine & Friends®

A BRITT ALLCROFT COMPANY PRODUCTION

Based on The Railway Series by The Reverend W Awdry. © 2006 Gullane (Thomas) LLC.
Thomas the Tank Engine & Friends and Thomas & Friends are trademarks of Gullane Entertainment Inc.
Thomas the Tank Engine & Friends is Reg. U.S. Pat. TM Off.

A HIT Entertainment Company

www.randomhouse.com/kids/thomas   www.thomasandfriends.com

Library of Congress Control Number: 2006922095

ISBN-13: 978-0-375-83465-3   ISBN-10: 0-375-83465-6
Printed in the United States of America     20  19          First Edition

Thomas puffed into the Yard after a long day. He saw
James and Gordon talking together. When he stopped at the
water tower, he could hear everything they said.

"I am too important to pull such an ancient load," said Gordon.

"Yes," replied James. "I am glad they brought that old bucket of bolts to do it. The engines here are all too fine."

"I'm surprised he can do *anything,* he is so old."

"Well, it makes sense for him to pull that Special. The fossils deserve each other," said James. Both of the engines laughed.

Thomas wondered what they were talking about.

Percy was waiting when Thomas got to the Shed.

"Did you see Stepney?" asked Percy. "Did you see what his Special is?"

"No, but I heard Gordon and James talking about it," answered Thomas. "They said it was a lot of old junk."

"I think it's kind of neat," said Percy.

"Don't let them hear you say that," said Thomas. "They'll tease you, too."

Thomas liked Stepney. Stepney was one of the oldest engines on the whole Island of Sodor. He had seen a lot and had interesting stories to tell.

Thomas' favorite story was about Sir Topham Hatt as a little boy.

One beautiful day, little Topham Hatt was out for a carriage ride with his grandfather. The horse was dashing through the countryside. Grandfather Hatt saw a rut in the road, but it was too late to swerve.

*CRACK!*

The carriage's axle was broken, and the horse ran off. Luckily, no one was hurt. But they were a long way from home.

Just then, Stepney, a brand-new engine, came chugging by. He was pulling a load of coal, so he didn't have any passenger coaches.

There was only one thing to do. Topham Hatt and his grandfather crawled up on top of the pile of coal. And off they went.

When they got to town, little Topham Hatt was covered head to toe in coal dust. He was very dirty. And so was Grandfather, so Mother couldn't be cross. They both laughed—and even had their picture taken!

Thomas always liked that story, and Percy liked it, too. It made them laugh to think that Sir Topham Hatt was ever that dirty.

The next morning, Thomas went looking for Stepney.

"Good morning, sir," said Thomas politely.

"Well, hello, Thomas," said Stepney with a smile. "What do you think of my Special?"

Thomas looked at the rock with some bones in it and at the old chest. He didn't want to hurt Stepney's feelings. "It s-s-sure looks old," he stammered.

"It's the oldest thing I have ever pulled," laughed Stepney. "It makes me feel young. The chest is full of gems from Rolf's Castle in the days of knights."

"This fossil is from the age of dinosaurs. It is going to be part of the museum fair at Tidmouth. And so am I, because I am *so* old," he added proudly.

Thomas thought the things seemed pretty interesting, but he remembered Gordon and James saying they were junk. Thomas didn't know what to think.

Just then, Sir Topham Hatt came to see the engines. "Stepney and his Special must go to Tidmouth for the museum show," he said. "But the hill to Tidmouth may be too steep for Stepney with that valuable Special. So someone will need to help push from behind."

"Push? I would not *push* a Special made of solid gold," said Gordon, "let alone that pile of old junk. I only *pull* Specials, and important ones at that."

"I don't think we should have to push that Special, Sir," said James.

Thomas did not want the others to tease him. But he saw that Stepney looked sad that no one wanted to help him.

"I will push Stepney's Special," he quietly volunteered.

"Thank you, Thomas," said Sir Topham Hatt.

"I appreciate it when engines prove that they are Really Useful." And then he gave Gordon a stern look.

Gordon puffed, and James gave a cheeky chuckle. "Better him than us," he said.

Thomas pushed the Special out of the Yard. He heard
James call out, "Don't let them mistake you for that old junk
and send *you* to the scrap yard."

All the way to Tidmouth, Thomas worried about what everyone would say about his old Special. He knew the children liked him, but would they think he was just an "old fossil" when he arrived with this "old junk"?

When they arrived at Tidmouth, there were already lots of interesting things to see. There was a butterfly tent, a petting zoo, and a frog exhibit. Thomas helped Stepney onto a special siding that allowed everyone to see the fossil and chest close up. But no one seemed to notice they were there.

And then Thomas heard one little boy shout with delight. "Look over there! It's Thomas! And he brought a dinosaur!"

Soon Thomas and Stepney were surrounded.
"Cool!" "Wow!" "Look at that!"
Thomas had never heard the children so excited. He was excited, too.

Sir Topham Hatt walked over to them. Thomas was surprised to see that he looked dirty.

"Good work, Thomas!" said Sir Topham Hatt. "I should have come with you and Stepney. I got a flat tire. I haven't been this dirty in a long, long time." He laughed. "Do you remember that day on the coal car, Stepney?"

"I sure do," chuckled Stepney. "You were a happy little boy, Sir."

"Just like these children. They will never forget this day."

"And neither will I," added Sir Topham Hatt.

Just then, a man with a camera walked up. He said, "Everyone smile and say 'steamie!'"

*Flash!*